𝒩abhanya 𝒜nd the ℒost 𝒫assage

OrangeBooks Publication

1st Floor, Rajhans Arcade, Mall Road, Kohka, Bhilai, Chhattisgarh 490020

Website: **www.orangebooks.in**

© Copyright, 2023, Author

All rights reserved. No part of this book may be reproduced, stored in a retrieval system, or transmitted, in any form by any means, electronic, mechanical, magnetic, optical, chemical, manual, photocopying, recording or otherwise, without the prior written consent of its writer.

First Edition, 2023

NABHANYA
AND THE
LOST PASSAGE

Aadya Gupta

OrangeBooks Publication
www.orangebooks.in

About Author

At just 8 years old, Aadya is a bundle of joy and creativity, living in Bangalore with her family. She immerses herself in a world filled with books, songs, and art. Aadya has a knack for storytelling and poetry, creating magical worlds with her words. Her infectious cheerfulness transforms any space into a haven of happiness, and she is always eager to forge new friendships. Aadya's zest for life and love for creative expression shine through in her work, making her a delightful young author to cherish.

99

Nabhanya is a 7-year-old girl. She loves all types of outdoor activities. She likes badminton, table tennis, dancing, football, swimming, etc.

The summer holidays were coming. Nabhanya closed her book and sighed. 'Mother, where to go these holidays?', she asked her mother, Nila. 'Not Sapar Nana's, I'm sure. It's too hot in Chennai now. Let me see, what about Ajja's farmhouse?', said Nila out loud.

Nabhanya exclaimed. 'Oh, I'll love it in Lachen', she said. Lachen was one of the towns in Sikkim, where her grandfather and grandmother lived.

Aadya Gupta

It was always snowy and frosty in Lachen, no matter what season. Nabhanya lived in Nepalgunj, so it was getting hot there. 'Well, if you want to go, you have to ask Appa. He is the only one who knows the climate of Lachen', said Nila.
'I'll ask Appa right away', said Nabhanya, and ran off at top speed.

Neeraj, Nabhanya's Appa, was a traveller and had lived in Lachen all his life. Whenever he was there, he focused on his hometown, gaining extensive knowledge about all aspects of Lachen.

Aadya Gupta

'Well,' said Neeraj when Nabhanya asked him about Lachen, 'the climate is worth it in this hot weather. You'll enjoy it there. It's so cold there. Your sunburn will be gone. But you will come back pale,' he said and smiled.

Nabhanya laughed and laughed, and now she was joyful. She loved her funny father. He didn't smile through his face but through his eyes. His eyes always twinkled when he was happy. His eyes twinkled right now.

'Ok, Appa, then it's settled. I can go to Lachen!' said Nabhanya. She went off to tell her mother.

Aadya Gupta

The next day, they set off for Lachen. The flight took off rather quickly. They reached Sikkim in 2 hours. Nila didn't come because she had some work in her hospital.

Ajja and Ajji were waiting for them at the airport. They took Nabhanya gently by the hand. 'Well, good that you've come here. We thought you were going to come late. You came too early. Let's go,' Ajji said.

'Bye, Appa! See you after 2 months,' yelled Nabhanya. 'Bye, Nabhanya. See you!!' yelled Appa.

'Come along, Nibha dear. You must be tired,' said Ajja, reading Nabhanya's thoughts. Nabhanya was sometimes called Nibha by her parents and family.

Aadya Gupta

There was a scooter waiting for them. Nibha sat at the front. Then came the sound of the motor, and they were off. In the middle, there was snowfall. As it was May, it was also a bit warm. So, they cuddled as close as they could to keep warm.

'Nibha, in Lachen, near our farmhouse, you'll meet a cousin of yours. I expect you haven't seen Nihil, have you?' asked Ajji. 'Oh, you mean Ajay Fufa's and Nayati Bua's son, Nihil Gotia?' asked Nibha.

'I heard about him. He sounds nice,' she added. They reached the farmhouse. There were green valleys and a few houses scattered along this vast corner. But Nibha loved it. There was a big house a few meters away. A boy came out of the stout door. He was dressed in a blue shirt with a slightly dirty black short pants. He had brown hair.

'Those are our friends and neighbours, Ajja Taman and Ajji Tammanna. And that's Nihil,' said Ajji, pointing towards the boy in the blue shirt.

'Nihil baccha, at least you can say hi to Nibha here,' said Ajja Taman. 'Oh, I didn't see her. Hello Nibha, do you want to pluck a few fresh and juicy cherries with me?' Nihil asked. 'Yes! And look at those juicy apples there, we can pluck them and eat them! And what about this vast jungle? We can explore it sometime.

Look at these beautiful valleys... let's go explore them... and these...', and off went Nibha and Nihil, best friends!

'Well, they can come back anytime... er... well... bye neighbours, we will tell you once these naughty kids get back!', yelled Ajja. They went back to the cottage.

'Ananta, can you help us now? Ananta, where are you... can you hear me Ananta?', asked Ajja, puzzled that no Ananta had come. Ananta, the maid, came at last, a very, very joyful, happy and funny maid.

Her kind of people were rare in Lachen. 'Oh, Appa Mahan, I was just checking the grocery list in the storeroom. How could I possibly hear you from there?' said Ananta, still joyful. 'And... by the way, we've got everything from the grocery list. No need to go down to the mountain today!' she added. 'Well, that's settled,' Ajji said.

'Oh, and here are the dear kids!' yelled Ajji. Nibha and Nihil got back cheerfully, with a bunch of cherries in their hands. 'Ajja and Ajji, we found some new friends today.'

'They are smart and swift people, I guess, because we had a mini-race and one of them won. Hey Nihil, I love Manya and Sanya enormously, right?', Nibha said and then stopped for a breath.

'Yes, I like them, but I think they're blunt. Not too smart. But I like Wanishka and Srita', said Nihil, both of them were having different opinions.

They washed their hands and freshened themselves. It was time for lunch. Nibha said bye to Nihil and set out plates. Just as Ajji was serving, Ajja came out with the daily newspaper.

He waved it in the air, and this was the signal for Ajji that something was wrong. "What happened?", Ajji asked, curiously.

Ajja said, 'See here! "Near some roads of Gangtok, a tree had fallen in the terrible rain conditions. It is broken halfway through the road and anyone can barely go to the other side ". That means terrible rain! We can't go back to Gangtok to meet Nibha and Nihil! No fun for them at all!'.

Nibha gasped. She had been looking forward so much to visit Gangtok. A few days earlier, the weather was so nice!

'Oh Ajja, can't we go? We only have to go by car, stay in the hotel, enjoy the view, and come back', said Nibha.

'No Nibha, we don't have that much money. We can't have so much luxury', said Ajji, sadly.

'Well, its unfixable', said a trying-to-be-cheerful Nibha. But no more did they hear because it pattered with rain!

Arushi and Mahika were running outside, looking for shelter. 'Arushi and Mahika! Come here!', yelled Nibha.

'Okay, Nibha! Do you have a light?', yelled back Arushi. 'Yes', yelled Nibha again. Arushi and Mahika came through the door. 'Namaskar Ajji Radha and Ajja Jyotish.

I hope you had a great day. Not like us, I suppose?', asked Mahika.

'Yes, my dear. We indeed had a bad day. But what were you guys doing out there?', asked Ajja.

'We had gone out of onions, potatoes, carrots, celery, milk, and, curd, and as you have most groceries, we thought to come out here', replied Arushi.

'The grocery store is too far away! We don't have a raincoat, so how can we travel from here to there?', added Mahika. 'Oh! You should have told us!'

'We have a raincoat, and we could have gone from here to Ramanujan Ratri Cottage easily,' said Nibha.

'We thought that you guys go running for 3 hours a day, so your legs might be tired,' Mahika said.

'Oh well, if you or any other just want groceries, then tell us one or two days before,' said Ajji, laughing.

'OK! We should better get going, otherwise Pratham's Uncle won't be happy!'

Pratham's Ramanujan, or Pratham Uncle, was a local school teacher. He taught two classes in the afternoon, two classes in the morning, and one class in the evening. He did not teach in a school but in his extremely spacious cottage.

His cottage had 7 rooms and 5 bathrooms, each with a tub inside. He had a big mat in his hallway, on which he sat while teaching his students. He had two big halls and was the most generous and thoughtful person in the whole village.

Aadya Gupta

It was lunchtime. Shabalep and Gundruk were served. There were hot momos with chutney as well. Bamboo shoots and Thukpa were also placed on the table. Nibha loved momos with chutney.

'Ajji, can you tell me a story tonight?' asked Nibha.

'Yes, my dear. I will tell you a story that you've never heard before,' said Ajji.

Nibha was so excited that she even forgot to eat her favourite meal.

The next day was not so rainy, so Ajji planned to introduce some people to Nibha. 'Nibha, today we'll meet some new kids. You would love to make strong friendships with them. Do you want to?' Ajji asked Nibha.

'Yes! Are they kids?' asked Nibha, excited. They went to see them. Ajja and Ajji took Nibha through a thin, narrow lane called Chakumandi Lane.

'This is Aisha. She lives in Delhi with her grandparents,' Ajja said. 'Hi Nibha! So nice to meet you! Where are you from?' asked Aisha, cheerfully.

'Hi Aisha, I am Nibha! So nice to meet you too! I am from Nepal,' said Nibha. 'Come on Nibha, I will show you my friends,' said Aisha.

'Ok!' said Nibha. They went to a place where there was lush greenery, beautiful flowers, and unique winged animals. There, they saw five more children.

One was fair-skinned, fair-eyed, and had deep brown hair. She was a girl. One had sunny skin, and golden hair, and looked really healthy. The other three were boys. One boy was fair-eyed, fair-skinned, and had dark brown hair.

One was like Nibha - medium-skinned, with dark black hair, and a merry mouth and expression. Nibha liked him. The other boy was like a good and healthy girl.

The fair ones were named Radhika and Avian. The one like Nibha was named Shubh, and the good and healthy ones were Advika and Ahaan.

'Everyone, this is Nibha. She is from Nepal,' introduced Aisha. 'Hi Nibha,' said everyone very cheerfully!

'Hey Nibha, wanna see the jungle?' asked Shubh. 'Yes!' said Nibha, and she felt warmth towards Shubh immediately. They went through the lush greenery and, surprisingly, came into the backyard of Ajji's garden.

'Ajji Radhalakshmi, can you take us to Kala Patthar?' asked Advika. 'Dear, Kala Patthar is too far. It is in Nepal! I'll take you somewhere else nearby,' Ajji said.

'Ok, Ajji. But where?' asked Avian. 'Just come, Avian! A surprise won't be worth ruining!' Ajji protested.

She and the children went through a narrow lane to a great waterfall. 'Now I'll leave you. Radhika, as you are the eldest, please take care of them,' Ajji said and went back.

'Ooh! What are those berries called in Nepali?' asked Nibha. 'They are called Sohphie in Nepali too,' said Radhika. But before she could even begin to say it, Nibha was near the bush.

"Careful, Nibha!' Avian shouted. But it was too late. She had gone. 'Maybe there is a secret passage!' Ahaan said. They went down to see. It was a passage indeed! It had strange carvings on its pillars.

Everyone was impressed by them. The passage ended. There was a door with a latch. 'Maybe it's locked!' said Advika. Avian just pushed the door, and it opened! They went in and saw that it was covered in moss and greenery.

There were objects made of gold, such as pots, necklaces, anklets, crowns, statues, etc.

There was a pond filled with water. There was something written on one of the left-side pillars. "When you drink the sacred water, Nandi, Ganesha, Parvati, Gauri, Saraswati, and others will rise. Out of them will come water, and the Saraswati River will come alive," Ahaan read in Nepali.

Avian was going to drink the water, but immediately Radhika said, 'No! We have to tell Nibha's grandparents before we drink the sacred water.'

They went back through the passage and ran back to Dream Cottage, or Samna Ramanujan Cottage. They ran at top speed to Ajji's puja room. 'Ajja, Ajji, we found a secret passage!' said Nibha.

Ajji and Ajja went to the place and agreed that it was sacred. 'I think we need to find good diggers and a strong and sturdy squad of villagers to help. We need to dig more to find out,' said Ajja as he looked at the deep hole.

'I agree. When I glanced around, I only saw Parvati, Ganesha, Gauri, and Shiva. Maybe the other gods are deeper down,' said Advika. 'What's the best way to find good diggers?' asked Avian. Everyone was thinking.

Then Nibha jumped and said, 'I know just the idea! We can call my dad and ask if he knows anybody who digs with a team!' Everyone thought that this was the best and most suitable idea.

Ajji called Neeraj after they reached home. 'Neeraj beta, do you know someone who digs to find artifacts?' asked Ajji to Neeraj.

'Oh yeah, there's Anju. She lives in Bangalore. She will come with a team and all tools! I'll call her right now if you want,' said Neeraj.

'Oh, not now! Call her tomorrow. We'll be ready by then,' said Ajji. 'Oh, sure Amma!' said Neeraj. They waited for Neeraj's team, but they also toiled a lot.

They found the perfect team to assist them. They were going to stay in an old, majestic house with all the services like pure water, maids, cleaners, puja rooms, and much more! Nibha and her friends also helped with this toiling.

Meanwhile, they learned a lot about the secret passage.

First of all, the water in it came from a very small glacier called Marantini, which flowed underground. Marantini was very pure.

'We have lack of water in our village. We can use the Marantini as our main source of water instead of the Lachen Tributary River. But one thing is that Marantini is somewhat thin and weak, even though it has the purest water in Sikkim,' said Advika.

At last, the team arrived. There were 30 people in the team, with 2 team leaders, Hiranjan and Dhriti, leading the team kindly and generously.

'Namaste, we were waiting for you since a long time, Hiranjan and Dhriti. We were toiling hard for you. There are Baburam, Harshith, Anjali, Bijoy, Pema, Pahya, Kashi, Tashi, Sophea, Mayuree, Adhiarja, Eshin, Komal, and Payal on our team to help with your people,' said Ajja.

'Woah! That's a long list! Let's start our work without wasting time,' said Hiranjan. While they worked, the kids found out a lot about the 30 people from Hiranjan and Dhriti's team.

Samya, a young teenager, loved making and inventing maps and ideas. Saumya enjoyed digging and exploring things. Amar had all the gears they needed. They found a letter while digging. Actually, it was a stone tablet that resembled a heading. It read, "Please note that the water from the kamal is not for drinking."

"It is for bathing all the gods and goddesses. You can drink the water coming from the gods and goddesses, but only after bathing all of them. The eldest one goes last. If many people are of the same age, the shortest one will go first," said Nibha.

"First, we'll have to find all the goddesses and gods. Then only we can bathe them and drink the water," she continued.

"And we have found the statues of Vishnu, Rama, Parashurama, Matsya, Kacchap, Varaha, Narasimha, Vamana, Krishna, Buddha, and surprisingly, half the statue of Kalki!"

"Then we have found otherwise Ganga, Shiva, Brahma, Saraswati, Parvati, and Mooshak. We haven't found Nandi, or others. Also, we have found unknown ones like Paranto, Karin, Poshrama, Sadandhitha, and
the mystery statue of Sarvapalli,' said Dhriti.

'Wow! We found out a lot, Dhriti!' says Nibha. 'I wonder where Gauri, Ganesha, and Nandi are,' says Avian. Then they worked really fast! They dug, dug, dug, and found Ganesha, Nandi, and Gauri."

Finally, they were done. Nila and Neeraj arrived just in time. 'Amma! Appa! So nice to see you all again,' they both said. Then they met Nibha.

Amma! Appa! Oh my! When, how, and where on earth did you know we were digging; and I thought that you would come!' said Nibha, cheerily.

People like Shubh, Radhika, Avian, and Ahaan burst out this time. They also knew Nibha's parents. They bathed the gods and goddesses with Nila and Neeraj.

At last, they had to drink the water. There were total seven kids. So, as Nibha was the shortest, she went first. She bathed all of the gods and goddesses and then drank the water after saying an Omkara. It was crystal clear, but, oh, so so so honey sweet. All other's mouths watered as they saw the crystal-clear water and then watered more as Nibha said, 'It's so sweet!'

Then it was Advika's turn, then Avian, then Ahaan, then Aisha and lastly Radhika. Everyone drank the water, and then it was time for Nibha to go. She said bye to everyone. Then the car zoomed off, and off went Nibha. But she will come back, and that's another story!

The End

www.ingramcontent.com/pod-product-compliance
Lightning Source LLC
LaVergne TN
LVHW061622070526
838199LV00078B/7392